1

Sunny the Sloth and Benny the Bear walk home from school. While walking home, they stop in front of Benny's parents' Honey Store.

"Benny, see you at school tomorrow!" says Sunny. "Bye, Sunny," Benny yells back.

Sunny walks through the rest of their small mountain town's Main Street. He looks in the window of Gill's Sporting Goods and sees the newest pair of Squirrelly Skis.

"Wow, what speedy downhill skis! I'll have the fastest skis on the race team! I have to get them!"

Sunny learns a lesson on spending...

2

Sunny slowly crawls home, worried about asking his parents for the Squirrelly Skis. While sitting at the table for supper that night...

"Mom and Dad, today I saw the new Squirrelly Skis in the window at Gill's Sporting Goods. My old skis just can't keep up. I really need them. Mom and Dad, can you please buy them for me?"

"Well, Sunny, we just bought you a birthday gift two months ago. However, now that you're 10 years old, we think you're old enough to start helping out around the house with chores."

"If you want those new skis, you're going to have to earn the money to buy them yourself, Sunny," informs Dad.

"We will create a to-do list chart. Everyday, you'll have chores to do around the house. It's really simple, Sunny. When you get your chores done, you cross it off. Some chores will need to be done every day, but some just once a week. That's why some will be worth only $0.25 and others are worth $1.00. We will pay you every Saturday for all the chores that you've done over the week."

Sunny agrees, even though he knows it will take a lot of time and hard work. Sunny really wants those new skis. He'll start the following morning.

Mom tells Sunny, "You will have chores to do before or after school. You'll have to decide to either get up a little earlier or do them once you get home from school."

Everyday Chores- $4.00 at the end of the week.
1- Make the bed every day. $1.00
2- Put dirty clothes in the laundry basket. $1.00
3- Put away all toys before bed. $1.00
4- Help set and clean off the dinner table. $1.00

Once-a-Week Chores- $1.00 at the end of the week.
5- Take out the trash and recycling. $0.25
6- Help carry in and put away groceries. $0.25
7- Vacuum the house. $0.50

· CHORES ·

★ EVERYDAY

1. FIX BED ♡
2. PUT LAUNDRY IN BASKET
3. PUT TOYS AWAY
4. HELP SET TABLE

ONCE · PER · WEEK

5. TAKE OUT RECYCLING

6. HELP WITH GROCERIES

7. VACUUM ·

12

A week goes by.

As he walks home from school, Sunny stops by Gill's Sporting Goods to look at the skis in the window. The skis cost $60.00, but he only gets paid $5.00 a week. Sunny figures out that he's going to have to save his allowance for three months before he can afford the new skis.

16

Sunny goes to bed feeling pretty disappointed. He knows ski season is just two months away and he won't have enough money to buy the skis before the first race. He thinks, "How can I earn more money?"

Sunny falls asleep as it starts snowing very heavily outside...

He wakes up and looks outside to see two feet of new snow! Sunny's mom yells, "Sunny we just got a call from your school... No school today; you get a snow day."

"Yes! Snow day!" shouts Sunny.

19

Sunny runs downstairs to grab his sled. He wants to go sledding with his friends, but as he walks out the door his mother yells, "Sunny, just one minute… Georgina just called and asked if you could help shovel since Gerry hurt his neck when he slipped on the ice. Will you help them shovel before you go sledding with your friends?"

Sunny makes quick work of the snow and helped clean off the sidewalk, driveway, and stairs all in less than an hour.

"Sunny, thank you so much for your help. It would have taken Gerry all day to do this. Here's 10 bucks."

"Thank you, Georgina, but you don't need to pay me."

"You worked very hard Sunny. You earned it."

Two more neighbors ask if Sunny could help shovel snow. He earns 10 more dollars before lunch time.

After lunch, Sunny catches up with his friends for an afternoon of sledding and snowball fights.

Two long months of chores go by. He knows by the next week that he'll have enough money to buy the skis.

"Sunny, I'm so proud of you. You've worked hard to save your own money for those new skis."

"Thanks, Mom! That was a ton of work! I'd better take care of these skis!"

Now Sunny learns a lesson on donating...

The next day at school, Florence the Fox is having a bake sale. Florence is raising money for the school's coding club. Sunny would like to support his friend and donate.

That evening, he asks his mom for a few dollars.

Mom says, "Sunny, now that you have chores and get an allowance, I think you can use some of your own money to help Florence and the coding club."

Sunny is sad that he doesn't have any money to donate to the coding club since he spent all of his allowance on the skis. So Mom steps in and helps him out this time. After, mom tells him how to "Save like a Sloth."

"Sunny, we are going to tell you the secret rule to afford everything in life that you want. You just need to remember to "Save like a Sloth." For every dollar you earn, you can spend $0.50, donate $0.10, and save $0.40".

Sunny learns a lesson on saving...

"Sunny, how much money have you saved?"
Sunny looks down and said, "Nothing, because I
spent it all on my new Squirrelly Skis."

"Well, every week you get paid $5.00, and
that's a total of $20.00 every month."

Sunny, you make $5.00 a week. Out of that
$5.00 you can spend 50%, which is $2.50. You
should donate 10%, which is $0.50. Lastly, save
40%, which is a total of $2.00.''

"Soon, you will have enough money saved to
buy whatever you would like and donate some
to help others in need."

Sunny frowns and says, "I only get to spend
half of what I make... okay, I'll try it."

Mom gets out three jars for Sunny. On each one she writes one of the three rules on how to "Save like a Sloth:" "Spend 50%, Donate 10%, and Save 40%."

A few days after buying the new skis, the newest pair of Hucking Hawk Skis are released.

Of course, Sunny wants the newest skis.

"Mom, can I buy them?"

"Yes, of course, but you have to save up for them first."

"Can I spend my savings on the new skis?"

"No. I'm sorry, Sunny, but that's only for really BIG purchases, like for your first car. You can also invest some of that money, but we can talk about that when you get a little older."

"For all the work it takes to earn a new pair of skis, I think my old skis will work just fine for now. Summer will be here soon, and I want a new mountain bike!"

Two weeks go by, and the coding club is selling baked goods again. Sunny is so excited because he's been saving 10% of his allowance to help others. The next day, he gives half of his donate jar to the coding club. He remembers Benny has a birthday coming up, and he wants to get him a birthday gift, too, with that money.

"There's nothing you can't buy when you Save like a Sloth!"

CREDITS

Written by Markus Heinrich
www.savinglikeasloth.com
savinglikeasloth@gmail.com
Instagram @savinglikeasloth
Illustrated by Nolan Schneider
Instagram @nolanart

Made in the USA
Monee, IL
14 June 2020